family picnic

ENDS

ST CARD

This space for Address on

scholar... Pfeffernut County. The...
fernut had high hopes for Louie.

Lost Toys Returned

Townspeople are delighted by the surprising
return of flying discs lost on rooftops and
kites tangled high in treetops. Balls and
other toys long since lost began to reappear
in the yards of Pfeffernut County children
a few weeks back. At first, no one knew
just how these things were being returned
from their high places. Then a local girl
spotted a lanky farmhand named Louie as
he plucked two baseballs from the gutters of
her family's home.

"I couldn't believe my eyes," she said. "He's
nearly as tall as the water tower."

"Aw, it's nothing," Louie said. "When I
see those poor toys stuck where most folks
can't reach, I feel real sorry. I can't help but
reach down and put them back where they
belong."

Please see LOUIE, Page A2

Greetings from Pfeffernut County

grandpa at fishing hole

Grandma's recipe

Pfeffernuesse Cookies - 5 dozen

4 C. flour
1/2 tsp. ground nutmeg
1/2 C. white sugar
3/4 C. light molasses
1 1/4 tsp. baking soda

1/2 C. butter
1/2 tsp. cinnamon
2 eggs
1/2 tsp. ground cloves
1/3 C. powdered sugar

Stir together flour, sugar, baking soda, spices + dash black pepper. Melt molasses + butter in saucepan, cool.

Stir in eggs, add dry ingredients to molasses mixture, mix well, cover. Chill for several hours. Place on Shape into 1" balls. Place on cookie sheet. Bake at 350° 12 to 14 minutes or until cookie done. Cool. Roll in powdered

The Cows Cannot Mooove Along

Pfeffernut County has not seen the sun for three straight days. Weather forecasters have no idea what's going on. The local livestock is completely frozen. Cows are no longer producing milk, just ice cream. Will this deep freeze continue, or will the sun shine down on Pfeffernut again?

Pfeffernut Book Fair $1

Pfeffernut Book Fair $1

LOUIE the LAYABOUT

by Nick Healy   illustrated by Sahin Erkocak

PICTURE WINDOW BOOKS
Minneapolis, Minnesota

Special thanks to our story consultant:
Terry Flaherty, Ph.D., Professor of English
Minnesota State University, Mankato

Editor: Christianne Jones
Designer: Tracy Davies
Page Production: Melissa Kes
Art Director: Nathan Gassman
The illustrations in this book were
created digitally.

Picture Window Books
5115 Excelsior Boulevard
Suite 232
Minneapolis, MN 55416
877-845-8392
www.picturewindowbooks.com

Printed in the United States of America.

All books published by Picture Window Books
are manufactured with paper containing at
least 10 percent post-consumer waste.

Library of Congress Cataloging-in-Publication Data
Healy, Nick.
Louie the layabout / by Nick Healy ; illustrated by Sahin Erkocak.
p. cm. – (Pfeffernut County)
Summary: People think Louie is a layabout but he really wants to do great
things, he simply cannot figure out how someone too tall for ordinary tasks
can reach that goal, until a farmer in Pfeffernut County sees his potential and
finds a way.
ISBN-13: 978-1-4048-3697-6 (library binding)
ISBN-10: 1-4048-3697-7 (library binding)
[1. Size–Fiction. 2. Work–Fiction. 3. Farm life–Fiction. 4. Self-realization–
Fiction. 5. Tall tales.] I. Erkocak, Sahin, ill. II. Title.
PZ7.H34463Lou 2007
[E]–dc22   2007004025

To Harrison – N.H.

WELCOME TO PFEFFERNUT

Pfeffernut County is a friendly little place on the prairie. It's full of kind people who dream big. Funny things have a way of happening here. Get ready for some new adventures, and enjoy your visit. We're sure glad you stopped by.

Louie was a large boy. He was much larger than the other children, larger even than his mom and dad.

Louie grew up in a small town. The town sat on a wooded hillside with tall pines standing all around. Only the trees were taller than Louie.

As a young man, Louie went off to work with his dad. Louie swung a mighty ax, but his aim was not always true.

"It's OK, Louie," his dad said. "We'll find another job for you."

Then Louie went off to work with his mom. He swung a mighty pick, but his aim was not always true.

"Don't worry, Louie," his mom said. "I'm sure there are lots of things you can do."

Louie wasn't so sure. He went home and whiled away his days. When summer came, he lay down on the cool ground under the pines. He rested like that for days and days.

"Don't be a layabout, Louie," his dad finally said. "You are big and strong. You can do great things."

"Like what?" Louie asked.

"I wish I knew," his dad said.

"I do, too," his mom said.

Louie decided to leave home, to go in search of a place where he could do something, maybe even something great.

He walked through the hills to the edge of the woods. Then he wandered along rivers and around lakes. He walked and walked for days.

He passed by towns he had never seen before.
He saw people he had never met before.
Children ran off when they saw him coming.
Louie only smiled and waved.

13

At last, Louie found a place unlike any he had ever seen. The land was open, and the sky was high. The summer sun was bright and hot.

He walked through fields of corn and beans. He stepped over small streams. He followed dusty roads.

14

Louie stopped near the edge of a small town. Only the water tower was taller than he.

"Pfeffernut County," he whispered to himself. "Sounds like a friendly place to me."

In town, some farmers spotted Louie on the street.

"My goodness," the first farmer said. "Who is that?"

"He's a giant," the second one said.

"Say," the third farmer said, "what brings you here?"

"I want to do great things," Louie said.

"Like what?" the farmers asked.

"I wish I knew," Louie said.

One of the farmers had an idea. He was an old man and not as strong as he'd once been. He figured Louie would make a fine farmhand.

The old farmer took Louie home. He told him he could sleep in the barn.

That's just what Louie did. He was tired from his long walk, and he went right to sleep. He slept for days and days.

18

The farmers stood in the farmyard. Louie's snores roared in their ears.

"Looks like you've got a layabout," the first farmer said.

"Wake him," the second farmer said. "Put him to work."

"I've tried," the old farmer said.

The other farmers shook their heads.

Finally, Louie rose. The growls of his stomach were even louder than his snores.

He began to eat. He munched many cobs of corn. He ate apples off the farmer's trees.

He even took the eggs from the henhouse.

When Louie wanted some water, he swigged from the stream.

The old farmer ran into the farmyard. He stomped his feet and waved his arms.

"This won't do," the old farmer said. "This won't do at all."

"Don't worry," Louie said. "I'll make it up to you."

"How?" the old farmer asked.

"By doing great things," Louie said.

"No," the old farmer said. "You will work."

And work he did.

23

The sun shone hot all summer. Louie filled his cheeks in the stream and sprayed the crops.

"Keep at it," the old farmer said.
"There is always another chore to do."

Crows came to feed on the corn. Louie clapped his hands and ran through the fields.

"Well done," the old farmer said. "Keep it up."

In the fall, Louie cleared cornfields. He tossed hay bales as if they were as light as feathers. He plucked apples from treetops.

The farmers watched in wonder.

"My goodness," the first farmer said.

"He does the work of ten farmhands," the second farmer said.

"Yes," the old farmer said. "Louie is no layabout after all."

When the work was done, Louie sat next to the old farmer. They watched the sun set over the empty fields.

"You were right," the old farmer said.

"About what?" Louie asked.

"You promised to do great things," the old farmer said. "And you did."

PFEFFERNUT FOLLOW-UP

1. Early in the story, Louie has a hard time. He wants to be like his mother and father, but it doesn't work out. Why do you think Louie decides it's a good idea to leave his family's home in the woods?

2. Louie travels from the woods to the prairie. Finally, he finds that he can be a big help on the farm. Why is the prairie a good place for Louie?

3. Louie doesn't look like other people, and his size makes life hard for him in some ways. Has there ever been a time when you felt like you did not fit in? Did that bother you? What did you do about it?

4. Louie's dad believes his son will do "great things" in life. Why does he believe this? Does Louie end up doing great things?

5. Webster's Dictionary defines layabout as "a lazy shiftless person." Was Louie really a layabout?

Fun Facts about farms, people, and land

• When settlers first arrived from Europe, nearly half of the land that became the United States was covered by forests.

• The term "tall tale" was first used to describe the stories shared by traders, lumberjacks, and others on the American frontier. Such stories often included exaggerations about people and their actions.

• People grow corn on every continent of the world except Antarctica.

• Each ear of corn has 600 to 800 kernels.

• It takes an apple tree four to five years to produce its first fruit.

• Robert Pershing Wadlow (1918–1940) was the world's tallest person, according to Guinness World Records. The Illinois man was 8 feet-11 inches (2.7 meters) tall. The tallest woman is Sandy Allen. She measures 7 feet-7 inches (2.3 m).

The series title, "Pfeffernut County," comes from the German word *Pfeffernuesse* (FEFF-er-noos). Pfeffernuesse are German spice cookies that are popular around Christmastime. They get their spicy flavor from ingredients such as cinnamon, nutmeg, cloves, and black pepper.

50¢ weekdays $1.00 Sundays

More Books to Read

Burton, Virginia Lee. *Mike Mulligan and His Steam Shovel*. Boston: Houghton Mifflin, 1967.

Carlson, Nancy L. *Think Big!* Minneapolis: Carolrhoda Books, 2004.

Mayes, Walter M. *Walter the Giant Storyteller's Giant Book of Giant Stories*. New York: Walker, 2005.

Shulman, Mark. *Louis & the Dodo*. New York: Sterling Publishing Co., 2005.

Sis, Peter. *A Small Tall Tale from the Far, Far North*. New York: Knopf, 1993.

Wallace, Ian. *Boy of the Deeps*. New York: DK Ink, 1999.

FactHound

FactHound offers a safe, fun way to find Web sites related to topics in this book.
All of the sites on FactHound have been researched by our staff.

1. Visit *www.facthound.com*
2. Type in this special code: 1404836977
3. Click on the FETCH IT button.

Your trusty FactHound will fetch the best sites for you!

Look for all of the books in the Pfeffernut County series:

Farmer Cap
Fawn Braun's Big City Blues
Henry Shortbull Swallows the Sun
Louie the Layabout

Greetings from Pfeffernut County

Grandpa at fishing hole

Grandma's recipe

Pfeffernuesse Cookies — 5 dozen

4 C. flour
1/2 tsp. ground nutmeg
1/2 C. white sugar
3/4 C. light molasses
1 1/4 tsp. baking soda

1/2 C. butter
1/2 tsp. cinnamon
2 eggs
1/2 tsp. ground cloves
1/3 C. powdered sugar

Stir together flour, sugar, baking soda, spices + dash black pepper. Melt molasses + butter in saucepan. Cool.

Stir in eggs, add dry ingredients to molasses mixture, mix well, cover. Chill for several hours. Shape into 1" balls. Place on cookie sheet. Bake at 350° 12 to 14 minutes or until cookies done. Cool. Roll in powdered sugar.

The Cows Cannot Mooove Along

Pfeffernut County has not seen the sun for three straight days. Weather forecasters have no idea what's going on. The local livestock is completely frozen. Cows are no longer producing milk, just ice cream. Will this deep freeze continue, or will the sun shine down on Pfeffernut again?

Pfeffernut
Book Fair $1

Pfeffernut
Book Fair $1

PFEFFERNUT

harvest time

School Book Drive a Colorful Success!

A small bet between the principal and students at Pfeffernut Elementary School has led to the largest book drive in the school's history. The students collected 1,000 books in just one week.

"We challenged our students, and they made us proud," the principal said. "Now I have to fulfill my part of the bet and dye my hair blue for the rest of the school year."

Pfeffernut Theater Grand Reopening

Main Street, minutes before the Theater's Grand

Downtown Pfeffernut looked more like New York City than a small town on Friday night. Bright lights glared, loud music blared, and huge crowds poured into the local theater to celebrate its grand reopening.

Last summer, a huge tornado destroyed the theater. Staying true to

Pfeffernut form, the owner picked a fitting movie to be shown at the reop "Twister." Please see THE

ADMIT ONE
Pfeffernut Theater

ADMIT ONE
Pfeffernut Theater

Local Farmer Gets Pilot's License

Farmer Cap of Pfeffernut County endured many hours in